The Ice Cream Swipe

I looked over towards the buggy. Then there was a horrible, horrible moment that seemed to last for ever.
The buggy was empty. Jamie had gone.

The last thing Gavin wants to do is take his little brother Jamie with him to the playground. It will totally ruin his image to be seen pushing a buggy, and anyway, he and Josh want to practise their synchronized swinging.

Gavin only takes his eye off the buggy for a minute—but in that minute Jamie disappears. The boys are convinced he has been kidnapped by a baby-stealing gang and rush off in hot pursuit of the most likely suspect—Mrs Parker, the ice cream lady.

Elizabeth Laird was born in New Zealand and has always had a burning desire to travel. She has lived in Malaysia, Ethiopia, India, and Iraq and met her husband on an aeroplane between Mumbai and Bhopal—and they have been travelling together ever since. When not abroad they live in Richmond, Surrey, with their two sons. Elizabeth has written many books for children, including a collection of Ethiopian folk tales, *When the World Began*. She has won the Children's Book Award and the Smarties Young Judges Award and has been shortlisted for the Carnegie Medal three times. *The Ice Cream Swipe* is her first novel for Oxford University Press.

The Ice Cream Swipe

OTHER OXFORD FICTION

THE ICE CREAM SWIPE

Elizabeth Laird

Illustrated by Ted Dewan

OXFORD
UNIVERSITY PRESS

OXFORD
UNIVERSITY PRESS

Great Clarendon Street, Oxford OX2 6DP

Oxford University Press is a department of the University of Oxford.
It furthers the University's objective of excellence in research, scholarship,
and education by publishing worldwide in

Oxford New York
Auckland Bangkok Buenos Aires
Cape Town Chennai Dar es Salaam Delhi Hong Kong Istanbul
Karachi Kolkata Kuala Lumpur Madrid Melbourne Mexico City Mumbai
Nairobi São Paulo Shanghai Taipei Tokyo Toronto

Oxford is a registered trade mark of Oxford University Press
in the UK and in certain other countries

British Library Cataloguing in Publication Data available

ISBN 0 19 275276 6

3 5 7 9 10 8 6 4 2

Typeset by AFS Image Setters Ltd, Glasgow

Printed in Great Britain by
Cox & Wyman Ltd, Reading, Berkshire

For Georgia, Barney and Emily

Chapter One

You know that game where you and your best mate walk backwards down the street, and the first one to bump into a lamp post, or a traffic warden, or a man with a mad Alsatian or something has lost?

It's brilliant. I'm best at it usually. I reckon I know all the streets round us so well I could draw you a map of the whole area with my eyes shut. Easy peasy.

The trouble is, my best mate Josh gets sick of playing it with me because I nearly always win.

'It's dangerous,' he said, last time I suggested it. 'What if you trod on a pigeon or a squirrel or something? There are loads of them round here.'

'Tread on a pigeon? Fat chance,' I said. 'You couldn't if you tried. They've

1

got instincts of self-preservation. They never let you get anywhere near.'

'Well, you might fall into a pond and drown.'

'A pond? In our street? You've been watching too many weird movies, my son,' I told him. 'Ponds don't just turn up in the middle of people's streets. The nearest one's in the park. It's miles away. Three streets, anyway.'

'OK,' said Josh, 'but supposing you accidentally go off the pavement and fall under a bus?'

'There are never any buses round here,' I said. 'Not when you want them, anyway. Me and Mum had to wait about three years for a bus last time we tried to go to my gran's, and Jamie was screaming his head off the whole time.'

Jamie's my little brother. He's two, and he drives me round the bend.

'Well anyway,' said Josh, 'let's go down the playground and have a go on the swings.'

'OK.'

The playground's in a corner of the park, through the side entrance, and up a tarmac path. It's not bad down there. Me and Josh go all the time.

My big mistake was to ask Mum if we could go. She was in the kitchen, sitting at the table, yawning her head off over a cup of coffee, and Jamie was sitting on the floor, muttering on and on to himself while he shunted a conker round the carpet, pretending it was a fire engine or something. I know. Pathetic.

'Go to the playground?' said Mum, smiling at me so hard I got suspicious straight away. 'What a good idea. You can take Jamie with you in the buggy. He's bound to go off to sleep. Up half the night, poor little thing, with his new tooth coming through. Kept me awake till half past three. If I don't have a bit of peace and quiet this afternoon I'm going to murder someone.'

'Take Jamie?' I said, backing away. 'To the playground? Mum, you've got to be joking.'

But she wasn't.

So that was it. That was my day ruined. I felt a sort of stone sinking down inside me at the thought of it. Who in their right mind wants to be seen pushing a kid around in a buggy?

Who needs people going, 'Ooh, look, there goes Gavin. He likes babies. Lost yer dummy, Gav? Where are you off to? Popping down the baby shop to get yourself some nappies?'

My blood was running cold, I can tell you. It doesn't take much to get them going at my school, and once they're on your back they never get off it again.

But I'd reckoned without Josh. He doesn't care what anyone says. Things just sort of flow off him. At school, they don't bother with Josh half the time. It's like they think it's not worth teasing people if they don't even notice. Anyway, Josh hasn't got any brothers or anything. He's an only child. Lucky him.

'Do you have to put him on a lead or

anything?' he said, looking down at Jamie in an interested sort of way.

'Course you don't,' I said, revolted. I mean, Jamie is my brother, after all. 'You stick him in his buggy and wheel it along.'

'Cool,' said Josh. 'Can I push?'

That's Josh. Never thinks about his image. Lives dangerously, on the edge, all the time.

There was no way out of this now, I could tell. Mum was already buttoning up Jamie's horrible little green cardy.

'Jamie's going to the park with Gavin,' she said, going all gooey. 'Lucky Jamie.'

He smiled his crafty little smile.

'Jamie go park,' he said. 'Nice cream van. Jamie wanta nice cream.'

'Oh, darling!' Mum was putting on his shoes (the ones with the hard toecaps that he likes kicking my ankles with). 'Ice cream makes Jamie all sticky. You don't want to get all sticky, do you, my precious?'

'Yes. Like ticky. Wanta nice ticky cream,' said Jamie.

Mum gave another gigantic yawn and gave in.

'Oh, all right. Get him an ice cream, Gavin. Anything for a quiet life.'

That is so typical. Whatever Jamie wants, he gets. He fancies messing up my day? He wants to go to the park and spend a fortune on ice creams? He wants to set me up to look like a total idiot baby-minder in front of all the hard nuts out there on the street?

7

No problem. But if I want a quiet afternoon, just going around with my mates, doing really cool stuff on our own—no chance.

Still, there was no point in arguing with Mum. Once she's made up her mind you can't budge her. There was only one tiny little ray of sunshine left, and that was the chance of an ice cream.

'What about Josh and me?' I said, holding out my hand. 'Don't we get ice creams too?'

She frowned, and plonked a couple of coins down in my hand.

'Small ones then,' she said. 'Go on, hop it. It's—' She looked at her watch. '—half past three now. Be back by five. Jamie'll be wanting his tea by then.'

'What about my tea?' I said, but

she'd already gone out of the kitchen
and was halfway up the stairs.

'Mind how you cross the road!' she
called down to me. 'And don't talk to
any strangers.'

Then she shut her bedroom door and
that was that.

Chapter Two

I felt really, really embarrassed, like there was a neon arrow pointing down at me out of the sky, with the words 'This boy is a loser' in flashing electric lights set all around it. And I wasn't even pushing the buggy. Josh was. He didn't seem to mind at all. He didn't even notice the couple of geeks on the other side of the road who were nudging each other (at least, I think they were) and laughing at us. He just went on pushing, and I could see he was thinking that Jamie was kind of cute.

'What's that he's singing?' he said, tipping the buggy right over on its back wheels so he could listen to the mush burbling out of Jamie's mouth.

'Don't ask,' I said. 'You don't want to know. "Ring a Ring o' Roses" meets

"Nellie the Elephant" meets "The Wheels on the Bus". I know he's my brother, but he's off his trolley half the time. Totally potty.'

A second later, I wished I'd kept my mouth shut.

'Want potty,' said Jamie. 'Do a wee-wee.'

I wanted to turn right round and run away.

'No, you don't, you little weasel. You just sit tight. We're going to the park, then you'll get an ice cream, then you'll fall asleep, if you know what's good for you.'

But Jamie was wriggling and going red in the face.

'Wee-wee!' he whined. 'Now!'

There was no help for it. I looked

11

up and down the street, saw it was
empty, thank goodness, and moved at
the speed of light. In about ten seconds
flat, I'd unstrapped Jamie, got him out
of the buggy and whipped him round
the corner by the bottle bank, where
there was a drain in the gutter. Even
Josh could see that we'd never live this
down, not for the rest of our lives, if
anyone saw us. He kept watch for me
on the corner, but when I'd buttoned
Jamie up again and got him strapped
in, and we'd started off along the road,
he burst out laughing.

'What's so funny then?' I said.

'You are. You ought to see your
face.'

'Nothing wrong with my face,' I said.
'It doesn't look as if it got squidged

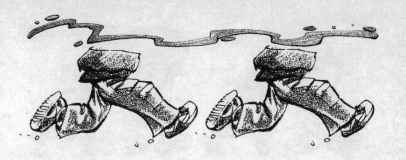

under a massive great boulder like yours does, anyway.'

I'd have tried to get his head in an armlock if we hadn't been stuck with the buggy, and we'd have had a nice little go at each other.

I could hear the chimes on the ice cream van ages before we got to the park. They got Jamie all wound up. He was bouncing around so hard the front wheels of the buggy were actually leaving the pavement.

'Oi, stop that,' I said. 'Sit down, Jamie. You'll tip yourself over. Hey, you've undone your straps. You cunning little devil. When did you learn to do that?'

I felt a bit worried then. I didn't know he could undo his straps. I hadn't wanted to bring the demon, but I didn't

exactly want him to run off and
disappear either.

Jamie didn't bother to answer. He
let me do his straps up, then started
fiddling round with the catch again the
minute I'd finished.

I wagged my finger at him.

'You leave those straps alone,' I said
sternly, trying not to take any notice of
Josh, who was still giggling, 'or you
won't get an ice cream. You read me,
Jams? I mean it. I'm not a soft touch like
Mum. You no touch strap, OK? You
undo strap, no have ice cream. Geddit?'

He pulled the corners of his mouth
right down, but he knew it wasn't
worth trying to make a fuss with me.
He might be potty, our Jamie, but he's
not thick.

14

Josh stuck his fingers into the ends of his mouth and eyebrows, pulled them back, crossed his eyes, and put his tongue out. Then he leant over the buggy to show his horrible face to Jamie.

Any other toddler would have screamed blue murder, but Jamie loved it.

'Josh gotta funny face,' he said.

'Not half as funny as yours,' I said. 'Look, there's Mrs Parker.'

Mrs Parker does the ice cream van. She's really old, and she's got this curly orange hair. She always wears masses of gold chains round her neck, and when she breathes in hard they jangle around on her chest.

When I was a little kid I used to

15

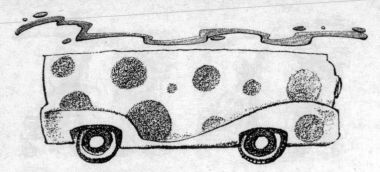

think Mrs Parker must be really rich, with all that gold stuff round her neck. Maybe she is. I don't know. She's made a fortune out of my pocket money, anyway.

'Hello, love,' she said to me, or it might have been to Josh, or Jamie. It was hard to tell. Mrs Parker calls everyone love. I suppose she sees so many kids she can't remember all their names.

'Two big 99 Flakes for me and my friend,' I said, sticking my money down on the counter, 'and a little one for the baby.'

Jamie was on to that in a flash. Trust him.

'Big nice cream! Wanta big nice cream!' he started bawling.

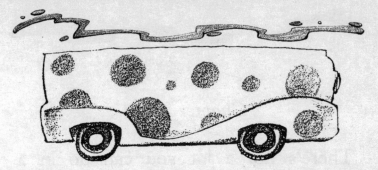

'Oh, go on, Gav. Have a heart,' said Josh.

I gave him a look. No loyalty, that's the trouble with friends these days.

No point in arguing though. I could see that Jamie was beginning to wind himself up.

'There you are, poppet,' said Mrs Parker, looking fondly down at Jamie and passing me a massive mountain of cold goo for him. 'That's right. You get stuck in straight away. Oops! Nearly dropped it. There now, aren't you clever. Ah, look at him. Always know what to do with an ice cream, don't they? Now then, young man, same again for you and your friend?'

Chapter Three

There's not a lot you can do in a playground with an ice cream in your hand except go somewhere and eat it, so Josh and me pushed Jamie over to the bench behind the see-saw. I'd had my fingers crossed more or less all the time since we'd left home, and I was beginning to think that we might get away with not seeing anyone we knew at all. Fat chance.

'Watch out,' Josh hissed suddenly, grabbing my arm. 'There's Hayley.'

It was too late. Hayley had seen us, and what was worse, she'd spotted Jamie.

Don't get me wrong. It's not that I don't like Hayley or anything. She's in our class at school and she's OK, really, with all the stickers and stuff she's got on her bag, and the way she curls her lips out when she laughs.

What I can't stand is the way she's so soppy. Get Hayley anywhere near a teddy bear, or a puppy, or worst of all a baby, and she goes totally liquid.

'Ooh!' she squealed. 'Wow! Is this your little brother, Gavin? Oh, he's so gorgeous. Oh, isn't he lovely.' She squatted down beside the buggy and poked Jamie in the tummy. 'Oo's a yum-yum itsy-bitsy scrumptious, then?'

I'll give this to Jamie. He can see them coming. He blew this massive raspberry at Hayley and drops of ice cream spattered all over her face. It didn't put her off though.

'Oo's a ickle-pickle sauce-pot naughty nibbles?' she cooed, fishing out a tissue and wiping down her cheeks.

She started gently pinching Jamie's

knees. Jamie kicked a bit, but he didn't smile. He'd sussed her already. Jamie may be only two, but he knows his rights, and not smiling at people like Hayley is one of them. It's not often I approve of Jamie, but I have to admit I did then.

'I'm going to take you home with me,' said Hayley, 'and you're going to be my little pet lambkin.'

That was when I had my brainwave. Maybe meeting up with Hayley had been a good thing after all.

'Here, Hayley,' I said. 'Don't suppose you'd keep an eye on him for a couple of minutes, would you, so me and Josh can have a go on the swings?'

Hayley was too busy to answer. She was gazing adoringly into Jamie's

horrible bulgy eyes. I know he's my brother, but he looks so like a frog you wouldn't be surprised if you found him sitting on a water-lily leaf in the middle of a pond. Honest.

'Just a couple of ticks, Hayles,' I said, gulping down the last bit of my cone. 'With a bit of luck he'll drop off in a minute.'

She nodded. At least, I think she did. Anyway, by then Josh was halfway across to the swings, so I said, 'I'll be right back,' and dashed off after him.

They're quite good, the swings in our playground. They're so high that when you get going you really feel like you're flying. Josh and I have tried out everything you can think of on

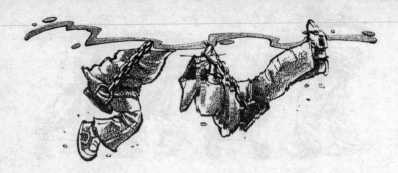

them—sitting down, standing up, twisting round, jumping off—you name it.

Our latest thing was synchronized swinging. You have to get both swings so they're going together, exactly the same speed and height, as high and as fast as possible. It's dead difficult. You have to practise a lot.

I didn't forget Jamie, though. I mean, I'm not that useless. I looked over towards the bench a couple of times and Hayley was still messing about with him.

Josh and I were doing brilliantly. We'd just got the swings up really high, and we were still together. Then Josh said, 'Hayley's waving at you, Gavin. I think she's going.'

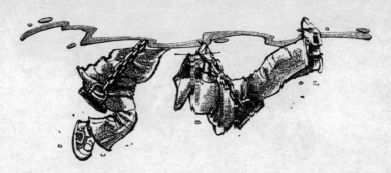

It was really, really irritating. I had to slow right down and ruin everything. Then I saw that Jamie seemed to be slumped down in his buggy, and Hayley was pointing at him and putting her head down sideways onto her hand to show he was asleep. So I said to Josh, 'It's OK. He's dropped off,' and we both started up again.

You do have to concentrate when you're doing synchronized swinging. I mean, it's quite tricky, especially if one of the swings is a bit wonky, and one of you is heavier than the other. I'm heavier than Josh, bigger anyway, and I reckon that made my swing go slower or something, so I had to keep my mind on the job if I wanted to keep up with him.

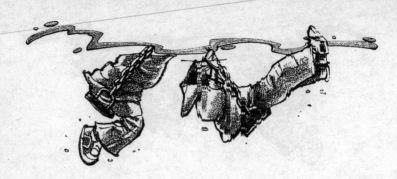

Most of my mind, anyway. I did glance over to Jamie once or twice. Once, anyway.

And then we got it perfectly. Really, really high and completely together, for at least ten swings. It's brilliant when that happens. It feels like you're in control of the whole world.

Then it started going wrong. My swing slowed down, and Josh's started going faster. We tried to pull things back together, but once you've lost it, you've lost it, so we gave up and came down to earth.

'What's happened to Hayley?' said Josh, looking round.

'She went ages ago,' I said, 'when Jamie fell asleep.'

I looked over towards the buggy. Then

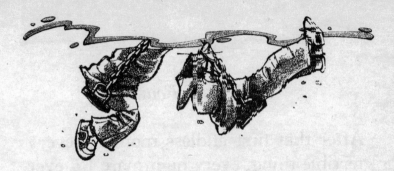

there was a horrible, horrible moment that seemed to last for ever.

The buggy was empty. Jamie had gone.

Chapter Four

After that first endless moment, every terrible thing, every nightmare I'd ever had, whizzed through my brain at the speed of light. What if Jamie had been abducted by a pervert? What if some sicko had taken him off and murdered him? I'd sometimes thought I'd like to murder him myself, but I realized in a flash that I'd never meant it. Not at all. Not one little bit.

The pictures in my head of all the things that might be happening to my little brother were so horrible that I felt my stomach heave. Everything in my head went sort of swimmy, the way it did last year when I got banged on the nose by accident in football.

I heard Josh say, 'Hey, Gav, you've gone a funny colour, sort of like lettuce. Did the swings make you seasick or something?'

'It's Jamie,' I croaked. 'He's gone. Look.'

Josh looked over at the buggy.

'So he has,' he said, all casual. 'Must have climbed out and gone exploring. He'll be around somewhere.'

I felt as if the earth had been heaving under my feet and it had suddenly gone back to normal again.

'Yeah,' I croaked. 'Of course. You're right. You look around this end. I'll do that end.'

It took us about twenty seconds flat to search the playground from one end to the other, and when we'd finished I got the sick feeling again, only worse this time.

'He's gone,' I said. 'Someone's nicked him, Josh. It's all my fault. I

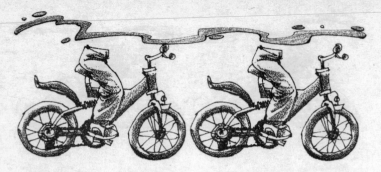

shouldn't have left him on his own. Mum's going to kill me. She's going to totally, totally murder me.'

When I said the word 'murder' I felt this lump in my throat as if I'd swallowed a whole egg, and my voice started going funny.

Josh was frowning, as if he was thinking.

'Hang on a minute,' he said. 'Don't panic. Look, those two guys over there by the gate, isn't it Marty and Pete? They'd have seen it if someone had come in here and gone off with Jamie. Whoever it was would have walked right past them.'

I was bounding across the tarmac like a kangaroo in front of a bush fire before he'd even finished speaking.

Marty and Pete are in the other class in my year, so I knew them a bit, but not that much. Marty was trying to do wheelies on his bike and falling off it all the time, and Pete was leaning against his bike, eating a Mars bar.

'Whassamattawidyou?' said Pete, whose teeth were all stuck together with toffee stuff.

I didn't bother to answer him. Pete's so slow it takes him half an hour to crank his brain up to answer if anyone even says 'hi' to him.

'I've lost my little brother,' I said to Marty. 'Toddler in a buggy. Did you see him? Did you see anyone come in here and take him away?'

I was talking so fast I was gabbling and even Marty, who's dead sharp,

was staring at me as if I was talking Chinese or something.

Marty stopped doing wheelies and sat back on his saddle, his arms crossed, staring at me.

'What are you saying?' he said. 'Your brother's been kidnapped?'

'Yes! No! I don't know!' I yelled. 'There's his buggy! Look!'

The sight of the empty buggy made Marty suck in his breath.

Pete unstuck his teeth with a sort of glooping noise.

'There was that kid with the weird hair,' he said. 'Bunches and bobbles all over it. Come to think of it, though, it was a girl.'

Marty was really concentrating.

'There were a couple of right little

pains chucking stones around,' he said. 'We had to get heavy with them.'

'Can't have been Jamie,' said Josh. 'There's only one of him and anyway he's too small to throw stones. He's only a toddler.'

He sounded so calm and sort of reasonable I felt like punching him.

'He's got to be here! He's got to! Babies don't just disappear, unless . . . '

My voice was shaking, so I had to stop talking. Suddenly, though, I knew what had to be done, and my voice went steady again.

'We've got to call the police,' I said. 'Who's got a mobile on them?'

'Me,' said Pete, looking all pleased with himself, and pulling one out of

his pocket. 'It's really brilliant. See this bit here? What it does, is—'

I grabbed it off him and tried to dial 999. Nothing happened.

'Battery's flat,' said Pete, taking it off me. 'Hasn't worked for ages.'

'Then what did you give it to me for?'

'You asked. You said, "Who's got a mobile phone?"'

I felt as if I was in one of those nightmares where you know you've got to get away from a terrible danger, but no one else seems to notice it, and they all keep blocking you all the time. Part of me wanted to tear into Pete right there and then and sort him out, and part of me wanted to just run away and disappear for ever, but I knew I had to stay in control. I looked at the

others. Marty had been feeling round in his pockets.

'Left my mobile at home,' he said.

'Mine got nicked,' said Josh. 'What about the call box up by the park gate?'

'Vandalized,' said Marty, spinning a pedal. 'It doesn't work.'

'That's it then,' I said. 'We'll have to go ourselves.'

'Go where?' said Josh.

'To the police station, you nerd.'

'You can't go down there,' said Pete, shaking his head. 'It's right next to the posh girls' school. Someone'll see you.'

'Pete! Shut up! Just shut up!' I yelled. 'This is a total, total crisis! My brother's been kidnapped! Someone came in here, into this playground, and picked him up, and smuggled him into the back

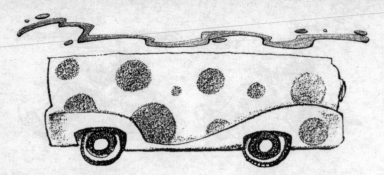

of their car, and drove off with him!
He might be . . . He's probably . . . '

I couldn't go on.

'No point in going down there
anyway,' said Marty. 'They've closed
that police station. They're pulling it
down. There's a new one somewhere
but I don't know where it is.'

Pete seemed to have got the message
at last. He sort of twitched all over and
stood up a bit straighter.

'The only baby I saw getting into a
car,' he said, sounding really sensible
for once, 'was the one climbing into
Mrs Parker's van.'

We all turned and stared at him,
goggle-eyed.

'Mrs Parker? She hasn't got a baby,'
I said.

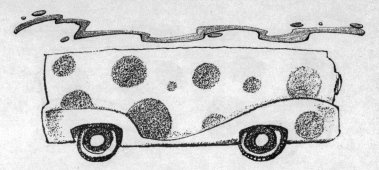

'Yes, she has. A little kid climbed into her van just before she went. She shut the door on him and went round the outside and got into the driving seat and drove off.'

I felt as if I'd been doing a complicated computer game, and all the graphics had exploded on the screen and put themselves together in a different way.

'This kid,' I said, and my voice was all hoarse. 'Did he look like a frog? Googly eyes? Evil smile? Covered in ice cream?'

'Didn't see,' said Pete, 'but he'd got a green cardy on. I noticed that because it looked like bird poo. I said, didn't I, Marty, "Look at that kid, he's been rolling in bird poo."'

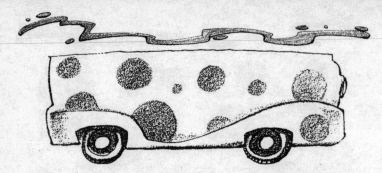

'Yeah,' said Marty. 'I'd forgotten, but you did say something about bird poo, come to think of it. I wasn't really listening.'

'That's him!' I yelled. 'That's Jamie! I don't believe this! Mrs Parker has kidnapped my little brother! Why didn't you tell me before?'

Pete dropped his sensible voice and put on his daft one again.

'You didn't ask me about Mrs Parker,' he said.

We all looked at each other, stunned.

'It can't have been Mrs Parker,' said Josh. 'Not her. She loves kids.'

'How do you know?' I was going frantic. 'Maybe she lures them into her van, with ices and lollies and stuff, then takes them away and sells them. Or

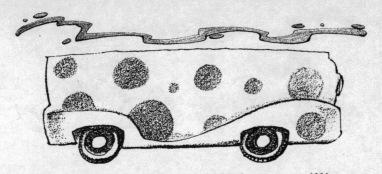

makes their mums and dads pay millions of pounds to get them back. Or gives them to perverts.'

I had a new picture in my mind now. Mrs Parker was holding out a lolly, and Jamie was staggering after it, his little hand reaching out and his bulgy eyes all shining and hopeful, and Mrs Parker was leaning down towards him, ready to grab him, her gold chains jangling. It was so real it was like in a film or something.

What did I know about Mrs Parker, anyway? I'd only ever bought ice creams off her. I'd never really thought about her, to be honest. She'd looked all right, kind of friendly and all that, really nice in fact, but they do, sometimes, don't they, weird nutters who steal kids.

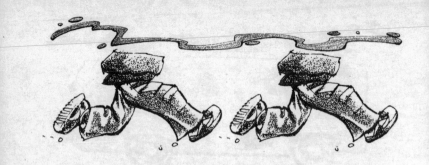

The more I thought about it, the more I remembered an evil gleam in Mrs Parker's eyes. And I was sure, too, that sometimes, when she'd smiled, her teeth had given out this starry kind of flash, like the baddies' teeth always do in cartoons.

I was beginning to see that there was a criminal plot here, and I reckoned I knew what it was.

'That's it,' I said. 'We were fools never to see it before. All that gold Mrs Parker's got round her neck. It's real. It's got to be! She's a multi-millionaire baby snatcher! Part of a gang! She grabs them and sells them on to other people!'

'Who, Mrs Parker? A multi-millionaire?' said Marty. 'I dunno. I

don't reckon that's real gold in those chains. My auntie's got loads like that. She gets them in Woolworths. They're dead cheap. Cheap and nasty, Mum says.'

'Never mind your auntie. Mrs Parker has kidnapped my baby brother. We haven't got time to mess about calling the police. We've got to get after him! Now!'

'It didn't look like she was kidnapping him, exactly,' said Marty. 'He just climbed into her van when she wasn't looking.'

'Yes. She probably didn't even realize he was in there,' said Pete. 'I mean, she didn't strap him into a seat or anything. Just closed the door and went.'

'She's cunning, that's why,' I said.

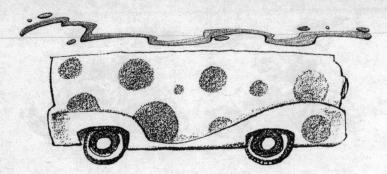

'She was trying to make anyone who might be watching think it was all an accident. She probably had a trail of Smarties running up the steps and into her van. Poor old Jamie wouldn't be able to resist.'

No one said anything for a moment. Then I smacked my right fist down into my left palm.

'She's not going to get away with it!' I cried. 'Whatever it takes, whatever it costs, we've got to get Jamie back!'

Chapter Five

The others just stood around and looked at me. I could feel my head clearing. I was beginning to see what had to be done. This thing needed planning. Organization. Leadership. Like generals do it in the army.

'What do you mean, get him back?' said Josh. 'How?'

'Now we know where Jamie is,' I said, 'we've got to get straight after him. We haven't got time to waste, trying to find the police station. We've got to hunt Mrs Parker down right away before she can sell Jamie on.'

'What do you mean, sell him on?' said Josh. 'Like Mrs Parker's a baby dealer or something? I don't believe it. Not Mrs Parker. I've been buying ice creams off her since before I was born. It's like Marty said, I reckon. She took

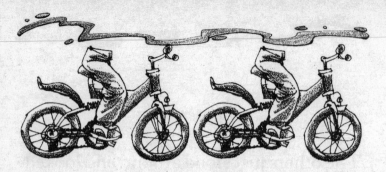

him off by accident. She didn't know he'd climbed into her van.'

That's the funny thing about Josh. He's amazingly casual about his image, but he's dead cautious when it comes to seeing the big picture and taking action. I decided not to take any notice. I'd got this new picture in my head of Mrs Parker now, and I just sort of knew it was right.

'Yeah, but supposing I'm right,' I said. 'We can't just let her go off and sell him. We've got to get him back anyway. We'll have to hunt her down.'

'Don't be soft.' Josh was shaking his head. 'We don't know where she's gone. She might be miles away by now.'

I was getting fed up with Josh.

'We'll ask people,' I said. 'Everyone notices an ice cream van. We'll just keep looking till we find her. The thing is, we need wheels.'

'There's my bike,' said Marty. He'd got a spark in his eyes now. He was warming up to it.

'And mine,' said Pete. 'Me and Marty will come with you.'

It would take more than a herd of elephants to put a spark into Pete's eyes, but I could tell he was trying, at least.

'There's Jamie's buggy,' said Josh doubtfully. 'It's got wheels.'

I gave him a look.

'My sister's over there,' Marty said, looking past us at a bunch of little girls by the see-saw. 'She's got a bike. I'll get her to lend it to you.'

'Gavin can't go on that. It's pink,' said Pete.

'Who cares what colour it is?' I said. He took a step backwards when he saw my face. One more crack out of him and I'd have strangled him. He knew it, too.

Marty dashed off to get his sister's bike.

'There's an old skateboard round behind the toilets,' Josh said, looking inspired suddenly. 'Someone must have dumped it there.'

'It must be bust then,' said Pete.

'No,' said Josh. 'It works. The wood's split at the end, but it sort of goes. I tried it out yesterday.'

'Get it,' I said.

A moment later, we had two proper

bikes, one little pink one, and a broken skateboard. And I had a plan.

'We'll fan out,' I said. 'Cover as much ground as possible. Josh, you're cool on skateboards. You go down the high street, along the parade, turn right and past the garage. Pete, you go round the church, in front of the station, and over the railway bridge. Marty, you check out the flats. There's often an ice cream van round there. Then come up by the cinema. I'll go right round the park and out the other side, then I'll whizz down the hill past the post office.'

'That's silly,' said Marty. 'We'll all end up at the bus station.'

'Exactly.' I nodded. 'We'll meet up there and report back.'

'What happens if one of us finds her?

45

Mrs Parker, I mean?' said Josh. 'How do we tell everyone else?'

'Yeah. Good point,' said Marty.

They all looked at me. That's the trouble with being a general. You've got to think on your feet.

'Observe the suspect's position,' I said, 'then leg it to the bus station and wait for the rest of us.'

'What if we don't find her at all?' said Pete.

'Well—' I stopped. I didn't want to think about it. 'We'll regroup, and make another plan,' I finished weakly.

'But it's miles round by the parade,' Josh said, shaking his head at the skateboard. 'It'll take hours on this thing.'

'We haven't got hours!' I realized my

hands had gone all wet and sweaty. 'By this time, Mrs Parker might have passed Jamie on to someone else.'

'Yes, to a pet shop or something,' said Josh sarcastically.

Pete thought this over. Then he shook his head.

'Nah, not a pet shop. They don't do babies. Wouldn't be allowed,' he said.

I rolled my eyes.

'Look, you idiots,' I began, then I stopped. There was no point in arguing. There wasn't a moment to waste.

'You've got ten minutes.' I looked at my watch, and my blood ran cold. It was gone four fifteen already, and Mum said we had to be back by five. The thought of going home with an

empty buggy, and telling Mum that Jamie had been abducted by the evil queen of an ice cream gang made me feel so wobbly inside that I had to give myself a good shake to get back on course.

'We'll meet at the bus station at twenty-seven minutes past four precisely,' I told the others. 'On your bikes, everyone. Or your skateboard. Let's go!'

Chapter Six

It's not my idea of fun, I can tell you, cycling round the park on a little girl's pink bike, but then it's not every day your brother gets grabbed by a millionaire maniac disguised as a nice kind lady with a sweet tooth. Luckily, I had my baseball cap on, so I pulled the brim right down over my nose and just hoped no one would recognize me.

Our park's on a hillside, and I went roaring up to the top so I could get a view of the whole place. I was panting so hard by the time I got there I thought I'd drop down dead. I was just leaning over those awful little handlebars to recover, when I heard them.

Somewhere, not far away, were the chimes of an ice cream van. They were playing 'Oranges and Lemons'.

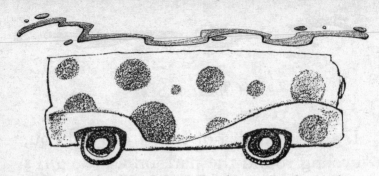

It can't be Mrs Parker, I thought. She always does 'Twinkle Twinkle Little Star'. Then it dawned on me. With fiendish cunning, Mrs Parker had changed her tune. She was covering her tracks, deliberately putting me off the scent.

I took off at once, and belted down the path on the far side of the park towards where the chimes were coming from. A couple of seconds later, I was in sight of the main gate, and there it was. An ice cream van. A little girl was holding up her money to the window, and a hand was passing an ice cream down to her.

'Watch out!' I wanted to yell. 'She'll grab you!'

But then disaster struck. Marty's

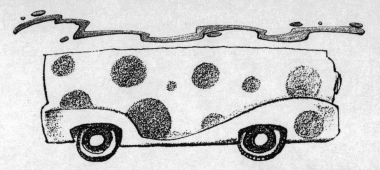

sister's horrible pink bike had really weird steering. I was trying to go round an old lady and her yappy little Pekinese dog, and I wrenched the handlebars too far to the right. The whole thing tipped over and landed me on the tarmac.

The old lady bent down to help me up, and the Peke's lead got tangled up in my front wheel, and my cap fell off, and the Peke pounced on it and started trying to eat it, and the old lady began clucking like a hen and pulling my cap out of the Peke's mouth. It took about a hundred years to sort it all out.

And when at last I'd got back on the bike again, and got myself to the park gates, that was it. The ice cream van had gone. Vanished into thin air.

To be quite honest, I nearly cried then. I'd managed not to so far, but what with the bash on my knee, and the van going and all, and the others not being there, I could just have stood and howled my eyes out and waited for someone to come and sort it all out for me. But then I thought of poor old Jamie, who could be stuck in a cage like a monkey by now, for all I knew, so I got back on the bike, shot out through the park gates and tore off down the hill towards the fire station.

I'd almost got to the fork in the road when I heard it again.

'Da-di-da-di-da-da.'

It was those old Oranges and Lemons again. But which way had the

van gone? Down the left fork, or down the right?

I was in agonies, trying to make my mind up, when I saw a flash of pink and yellow. The ice cream van had gone down the left fork, and now it was way down the bottom of the hill, pulled up at the traffic lights.

I rode down the hill so fast I swear the wheels of that bike never touched the tarmac. Cats and traffic wardens and old guys crossing the road with walking sticks had to dive for the pavement to get out of my way.

Even so, I got there too late. When I reached the traffic lights, the ice cream van had disappeared off the face of the earth. Out of sight, anyway.

Just then, I caught sight of the clock

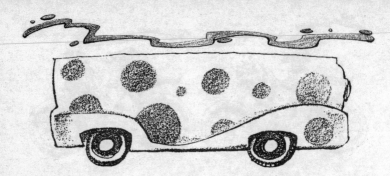

that hangs out over the street above the front of the jeweller's shop. 4.28! I was a minute late already!

I leaned forward over the handlebars and started to pedal furiously towards the bus station.

And then it happened. I was going past the last row of shops, feet pumping, gasping for breath, when, bold as brass, the ice cream van came up from behind, out of nowhere, and sailed right past me.

'Oi!' I shouted at the top of my voice, not caring that people were stopping to stare at me. 'Stop! Give me back my brother!'

But the driver didn't hear, and the van went careering on, spurting a disgusting cloud of black fumes into my face as it went past.

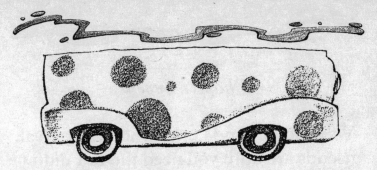

It turned left ahead of me, and I gave a squawk of triumph. It was heading for the bus station. Right into our trap.

Chapter Seven

You don't find out who your real friends are until you need them. I didn't realize that Pete and Marty were really good mates until that moment. To be honest, I hadn't even been sure they were going to turn up again at all.

I raced into the bus station, riding that little pink horror as fast as it would go. The ice cream van had pulled up just beyond it, on the far side, in a parking space behind a row of advertisement boards.

I was scared all of a sudden. I didn't want Mrs Parker to see me until I had my troops alongside me, sort of thing, so I looked round for the others.

I caught sight of Marty and Pete, or their bikes anyway, at once. They were huddled up behind one of the bus shelters, with just the front wheels of the bikes sticking out.

I dashed over to them.

'What are you hiding in here for?' I said. 'Look, the van's over there. We've got it cornered.'

'We're waiting for you,' said Marty.

'We're doing like you said. Regrouping,' Pete said. It was a long word for him, but I could tell he was trying. He was looking worried, too. 'We're being careful in case she gets violent. I mean, there might be a whole gang of them in that ice cream van.'

I looked out from behind the shelter and scanned the bus station.

'Where's Josh?'

'Dunno.' Marty was looking out too. 'Wait a minute. Yes! Over there!'

Josh was hobbling towards us, dodging between two buses, with the skateboard

under his arm. He saw us and limped across to join us.

'This thing's total, total rubbish,' he said, throwing the skateboard down on the ground. 'I fell off it about ninety-five times. I think I've broken my ankle.'

'Is it swollen?' Marty squatted down to look. 'We did bones in first aid last week. It all swells up if you've bust it.' He gave the ankle a prod, and Josh yelped. 'Nothing wrong with that. You've ricked it, that's all.'

'Ricked it? That's all?' Josh began indignantly.

'Shut up, you lot.' I couldn't believe they were going on like this. 'We're trying to rescue Jamie, remember?'

'Yeah, I know, but . . . '

Pete's mind was working; that is, if

you could call what's in his head a mind. You could practically see the wheels turning, anyway.

'But what, Pete?' said Marty patiently.

'What if she's got a gun?'

'A gun? Are you crazy?' I said. Even in my scariest thoughts I couldn't see Mrs Parker with a gun. 'I mean, think about it.'

We all thought about it.

'OK, men,' I said at last. 'Lock up your bikes and follow me. This is it.'

I've got to admit, though, that I did feel dead scared, marching across the endless, grey, windswept, empty, oily, bare tarmac. (Well, it was bare except for a couple of 127 buses and a 43, revving up for take-off.)

What if Pete was right? I still

couldn't see Mrs Parker herself with a gun, but what if it wasn't just her in the van, but a whole gang of baby-snatchers? This thing could be big, much bigger than even I'd suspected. The ice cream business could just be a front, and these people could be hardened gangsters, like the Mafia or something, and dead cunning, and they'd probably already spotted us, and were even now lying in wait, ready to make a sortie. There could be dozens of them in there, all of them armed to the teeth.

We should have got some back-up, I thought. We should have found another call box and dialled 999.

I put up my hand to stop the others, and they almost ran into me, except for

Josh, who was limping along at the back.

'In case of trouble,' I said, 'I'll go in front. He's my brother, after all. If anything happens, Pete and Marty can find another call box and get the police to send reinforcements. Josh's a casualty, walking wounded, so . . . '

'Limping wounded,' said Josh.

'Yeah. Whatever. So Josh stays here and just shouts as loud as he can to attract attention. *Capische?*'

'*Capische?* What's it mean?' said Pete, looking fogged.

'It means geddit. It's what Mafia bosses say,' Marty told him impatiently. 'Don't you learn anything at school?'

There was no time for more. I knew that it was now or never.

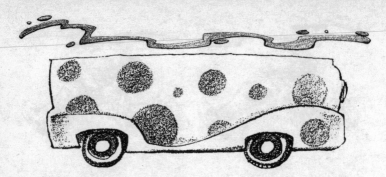

The advertisement boards between the bus station and the parking place half hid the ice cream van. We couldn't see it properly, not even to tell if the serving hatch was open.

We'd reached the nearest board, and were just regrouping behind it, ready for the final push, when the van's chimes suddenly blared out, making us nearly jump out of our socks.

We stared at each other, not knowing what to think. The van wasn't playing 'Oranges and Lemons', or even 'Twinkle Twinkle Little Star'. It was doing 'Girls and Boys Come Out To Play'.

'Hm. Very cunning,' said Marty.

'It's a smokescreen,' said Josh.

'A what?' said Pete.

'Shut up,' I said.

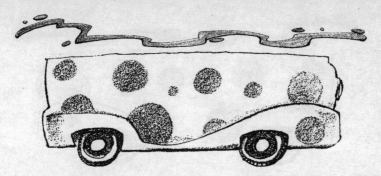

Cautiously, one after the other, we stuck our heads round the edges of the advertisement board and looked at the van. It was a horrible, horrible moment. Instead of Mrs Parker, with her orange hair and jangly necklaces, there was this human bulldog.

You'd know what I mean if you'd seen him. He didn't have a neck, so his head was stuck straight down onto his shoulders. His mouth was long and droopy, and his bottom teeth stuck out and upwards over his top lip.

The other three ducked back behind the board, but I knew what I had to do, and I did it. My knees were knocking, though, when I walked out from under cover and went up to him.

'Excuse me,' I said. 'Where's my

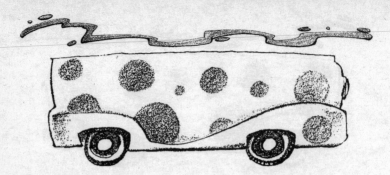

brother? Have you got him in there? Because I want him back.'

It was either that I wasn't speaking very loudly, or that a couple of buses went roaring past at that moment. Whichever it was, he didn't hear me.

'A Calypso you wanted, was it?' he said, cupping his hand behind his ear. 'My personal favourite too. Coming up, my lad.'

His voice wasn't what I'd expected at all. It was normal, and really nice. Just ordinary and friendly. And when I looked at him again, I could see that though he still looked like a bulldog, it was like one of those friendly, soft ones, the sort that people don't mind taking along with them when they go to feed the ducks in the park with the baby.

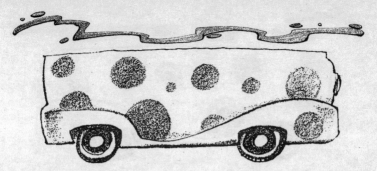

I nearly said, 'Calypso? Yes, please,' forgetting all about the ice cream I'd had earlier on, and my hand was going down into my pocket to fish out some money, when I realized Marty was standing beside me.

'Where's Mrs Parker?' he demanded sternly.

'Mrs Parker?' The man shook his massive head. 'I don't know. Up by the playground, that's her pitch. What do you want her for, anyway? My ice cream not good enough for you?'

'Yes, but she left the playground, didn't she?' I was pulling myself together, trying to sound meaningful and hard. 'She left suddenly. *Very* suddenly.'

'What are you on about?' the man

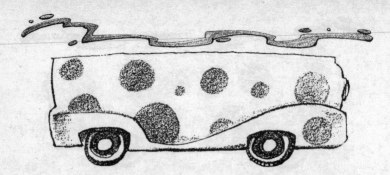

said. 'She's probably gone back home. Everyone needs a break sometimes. Worried about her cat, probably. It had kittens last week. She might have gone home, then turned round and gone back up to the playground. She's probably up there now. Look, do you kids want ice creams or not?'

'Well...' said Marty, looking longingly at the pictures on the side of the van.

'No,' I said, dragging him away. 'But thanks all the same.'

Chapter Eight

A minute later, we were back with the bikes behind the shelter.

'He might have been one of the gang,' Pete was saying. 'You can't ever tell. Just because he sounded nice and everything doesn't mean he's not a criminal hit-man. He might have had Jamie tied up in there, right under your noses.'

'He didn't,' said Josh.

Pete turned to gawp at him.

'How do you know?'

Josh looked triumphant.

'Because I looked, didn't I? While Marty and Gavin were talking to the guy, and you—' he frowned at Pete '—were standing there looking like a rabbit with half a brain, I sneaked round the back of the van. The door was open, a bit, and I got a good view

of the whole inside. There's no way Jamie's in that van. It's so full of stuff you couldn't hide a gerbil in there, never mind a kid the size of Jamie.'

'Gerbils can hide anywhere,' objected Pete. 'Mine keeps getting under the floorboards.'

I'd stopped listening to them. I was thinking things out.

'You heard him, that man,' I said at last. 'He reckons Mrs Parker has gone back to the playground.'

'She might have done.' Marty looked thoughtful. 'If she didn't know Jamie was in her van, and she found him there, she'd want to find someone to give him back to and the playground's the first place she'd look.'

'Or,' chipped in Pete, 'she's already

passed Jamie on to the next person in the gang, and now she's gone back up there to stock up on more kids.'

He smiled round at us, looking really pleased with himself.

'Whichever,' I said, looking nervously at my watch. 'It's 4.45 already. There's no time to hang about. It's on your bikes, everyone.'

'What bike?' said Josh gloomily. 'I can't even walk on this ankle, and don't think I'm ever having anything more to do with that skateboard, because I'm not.'

'Hop on the bus then,' said Marty, suddenly inspired. 'The playground's only two stops away and the 43 goes right past the gate.'

It was no joke getting back up the

steep hill to the playground on that horrible little pink object, I can tell you. First of all, Pete and Marty overtook me on their nice big bikes, and then Josh whizzed past in the 43 bus, waving at me like a flaming film star.

In the end, I got off the bike and ran for it, pushing it alongside me. I was so dead worried about time racing on, and thinking that I'd never get poor old Jamie back, and how I was quite fond of him really, and how upset Mum would be if we never saw him again, that I had that enormous great egg stuck in my throat again and the harder I tried swallowing it the more it wouldn't go away.

My superhuman efforts paid off,

because in the end I was only a couple of minutes behind the others. The three of them were standing on the tarmac path leading to the playground. They looked kind of tense, as if something scary was about to happen.

It was. Coming towards us, lurching from side to side with its headlights blazing, was a yellow and pink ice cream van, and from the loudspeaker on its roof came a terrible sort of wailing noise, that could, if you listened carefully enough, be the first few notes of 'Twinkle Twinkle Little Star'.

'Told you,' said Pete, backing away. 'It's a gang. The whole lot of them, guns, rockets, you name it. Face it, Gavin, we can't take this lot on. I'm out of here.'

He started climbing back on to his bike, and was just about to zip off when Marty grabbed hold of his handlebars.

'Look,' he said.

The van had stopped. The door was opening. And coming out of it, instead of the bunch of baby snatchers with balaclava helmets on their heads and machine guns in their hands, that Pete was obviously expecting, was Mrs Parker, holding my brother Jamie.

Chapter Nine

I let out a shriek that they probably heard in China. I let Marty's sister's pink bike crash to the ground and leaped forward.

'Jamie!' I said. 'It's me, Gavin! Don't panic! I'm going to rescue you.'

But Jamie didn't look as if he wanted rescuing at all. He had this happy grin on his face and he was chewing.

Then I noticed that Mrs Parker was holding him away from her nice clean pink jumper at arm's length, and that he was in the most disgusting mess that any toddler in the history of the world has ever got himself into.

He looked as if he'd been plastered with bird poo (to be fair, he couldn't help that—it was just his green cardy), then rolled in white and pink ice cream, then dusted with bits of wafer, then had

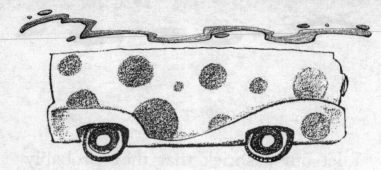

his face painted with melted chocolate and been decorated all over his hair with half-chewed Smarties.

He was awesome.

'Is this yours?' said Mrs Parker, looking at me with a desperate kind of hope in her eyes.

'Er, yes,' I said. 'It's my brother Jamie.'

Mrs Parker seemed to go soggy at the knees. She put Jamie down and he staggered over towards me, then sat down plump in the muddy flowerbed beside the path.

She'd gone a funny colour.

'I've been on the ice cream for fifteen years in this town,' she said, 'and never once, not even when a bus hit my van from behind and nearly turned me

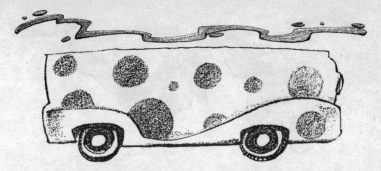

over, not *once*, have I seen devastation like this. Just look.'

She walked round to the back of the van and opened the door. Marty and Pete and Josh and me crowded round to look inside.

It was unbelievable. The floor was swimming in melted ice cream; pink, and white, and brown. Dribbles of it were running down the walls. Bits of biscuity cones were trampled into the mess and ground up with fragments of chocolate flake. The whole revolting mess was studded all over with sweets in sparkly wrappers, half undone.

'Cor!' we all said together. There was nothing else to say.

'I had to go home,' said Mrs Parker, to no one in particular, as if she was

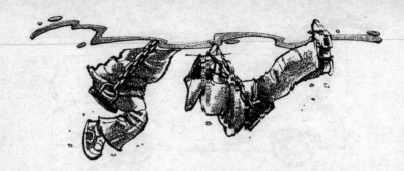

telling her story to the world's press. 'I'd forgotten to feed the cat, see? She's extra hungry at the moment, what with her kittens and all. I shut the van door and drove off. Never thought to look inside. I got home and gave Tickles her dinner, then when I went out to the van again I heard this funny noise. Like . . . like a sort of snuffling.'

'Same as a piglet,' I said, pleased to think I knew just what she meant. 'He often makes a noise like that.'

Jamie burped. His tummy was as bulgy as his eyes now, and he was picking up dollops of mud in his hands.

'When I opened the door of my beautiful clean van, and saw this . . . this creature . . . '

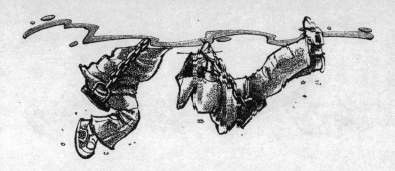

Mrs Parker shut her eyes, as if the memory was too much for her.

'I know. I often feel like that when I look at Jamie.' I was beginning to feel really sympathetic towards Mrs Parker. I couldn't believe that only five minutes ago I'd thought she was the evillest person in the world.

'And then,' said Mrs Parker, shuddering, 'I realized that it was a child. A poor little lost baby.'

We all looked at Jamie again. The description didn't fit, somehow. Pete and Marty were shaking their heads, and Josh was sucking air disbelievingly through his front teeth.

'And I thought of his mummy,' said Mrs Parker, looking almost tearful, 'and how she must be going crazy,

worrying about him, poor little soul, and how everyone would think he'd been kidnapped, and the police would be after me, and no one would believe me, and my licence would get taken away, and . . .'

She was shaking her head, as if she wanted to get rid of the horrible thoughts in her mind, and her orange hair wobbled like a great big mass of candy floss, and her chains jangled and jiggled about on her chest.

'We did think he'd been kidnapped,' said Pete, looking a bit disappointed, 'by a gang of baby-snatchers with guns and stuff.'

'You did,' Marty said scornfully. 'I never did.'

'And we were going to tell the police

but we couldn't find a telephone,' said Josh.

Mrs Parker let out a sigh of relief in a huge big gust. Then, floating up over the trees of the park, came the chimes of the town hall clock.

'Five o'clock!' I said, jumping with fright. 'I've got to get Jamie home!'

Mrs Parker was staring into her van, her shoulders drooping.

'Do you want us to help you clear it all up?' I said anxiously. 'Only Mum said . . .'

She shook her head firmly.

'Thanks, but no thanks. This is a job for the garden hose. It was my fault anyway. I shouldn't have left the door open.'

'And mine,' I said, feeling noble, and

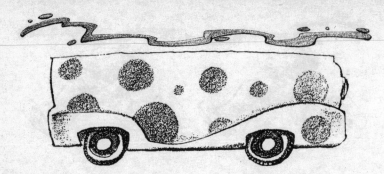

trying to cheer her up. 'I should have kept more of an eye on him.'

Mrs Parker shut the van's back door, hiding all the mess, and climbed up into the driving seat. Jamie looked up at her, and waved his hand.

'Bye bye,' he said, smiling all over his filthy face. 'Nice lady. Nice van. Nice cream.'

Something that could have been a grin broke out on Mrs Parker's face, and she shook her head at him.

'Kids,' she said.

There was a fizzing noise, and bubbles appeared round Jamie's mouth.

'He's blowing you a kiss,' I said.

Mrs Parker burst out laughing.

'Oh well,' she said. 'You live and learn,' and she blew him a kiss back.

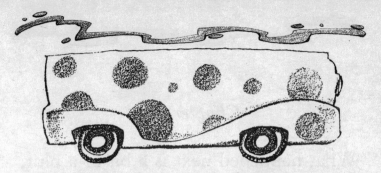

The van took off, and disappeared through the gates of the park.

The four of us stood in a circle and looked down at Jamie.

'You know what,' said Josh admiringly, 'he's a one-off.'

'A total disaster area,' said Marty, nodding. 'Completely septic.'

'A phenomem—phonemeny—pho-menen—phenomen—you know what I mean,' said Pete.

For the first time in my life, I felt really proud of my little brother.

'Jamie,' I told him, 'you are one evil baby. Come on. We've got to get you home.'

Chapter Ten

What happened next is a bit of a blur, when I try to remember it, because I was moving faster than a rocket going into orbit.

In about ten seconds flat, I'd given Marty's sister back her bike, and explained about the little dent in the mudguard being caused by the Peke in the park (she was really nice about it), found Jamie's buggy under a bench (luckily no one had nicked it while we'd been gone), told my troops that they all deserved medals for exceptional bravery in the line of duty, gone to the toilets and got masses of paper to clean Jamie up (I only made him look worse), said goodbye to Pete and Marty, and set off with Josh down the road towards home as fast as if a hungry lion was chasing us.

It was only ten past five when we burst in through the back door.

'Sorry we're late, Mum,' I said.

She was undoing a packet of chicken nuggets, ready for the microwave.

'Oh, are you?' she said. 'I lost track of time. Was it nice, down at the park? How's my little Jamie then?'

I held my breath, waiting for her to notice the unbelievable state of her youngest child, but she's so used to him she didn't even blink.

She bent down to undo his straps, then straightened up.

'Bless him,' she said. 'Fast asleep. I told you he'd go off, didn't I? I can tell he enjoyed his ice cream. Bit mucky, isn't he? Never mind. It all comes off in the bath. I don't

know how he gets himself in such a
state.'

I was looking at the ceiling.

'Nor do I, Mum,' I said. 'I can't
imagine.'

'I can't either,' said Josh, who was
standing by the door.

Mum gave me a little hug.

'Thanks for taking him along with
you, Gavin,' she said. 'No trouble, was
he?'

I was backing away, out of the
kitchen door, and Josh was sidling after
me.

'Trouble?' I said. 'Oh no, Mum. He
was no trouble at all.'

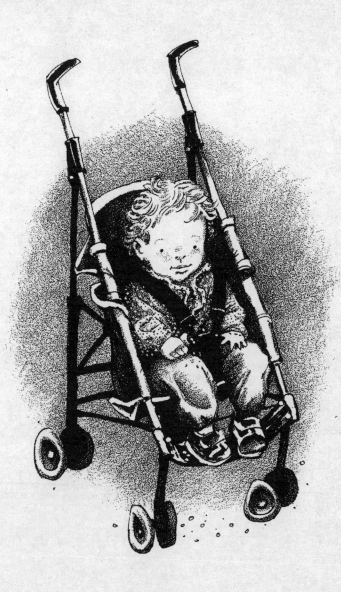